For I & M
- J. H.

A Lou, Paula et Johan mes super futurs voisins,
et Flora qui j'espère les rejoindra
- L. L.

tiger tales
5 River Road, Suite 128, Wilton, CT 06897
Published in the United States 2019
Originally published in Great Britain 2019
by Little Tiger Press Ltd.
Text copyright © 2019 Jess Hitchman
Illustrations copyright © 2019 Lili La Baleine
ISBN-13: 978-1-68010-172-0
ISBN-10: 1-68010-172-2
Printed in China
LTP/2700/2639/0219

For more insight and activities, visit us at www.tigertalesbooks.com

In Every House, on Every Street

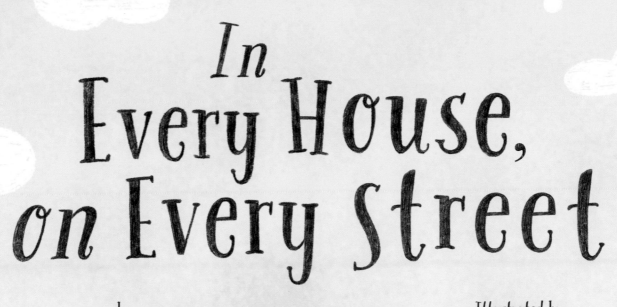

by
Jess Hitchman

Illustrated by
Lili La Baleine

tiger tales

Our house is made out of four walls and a door,
some crooked old bricks, and a creaky old floor.

But I've got a secret. Come this way with me!
I'll show you some things that you can't always see.

In this room we bake,
but we never **just bake . . . .**

We sing into spoons and get covered in cake!

We dance in our aprons and taste what we make.
We work as a team when we're learning to bake.

In this room we eat,
but we never **just eat** . . . .

We party like **pirates** and hunt for a treat!
We climb under tables and tickle some feet.
We share lots of giggles
each time that we eat.

In this room we chat,
    but we never **just chat** . . . .
We dress up like rock stars and sing to the cat!
We play silly games, but it's more than just that.
We say how we're feeling at home when we chat.

In this room we rest,
but we never **just rest** . . . .
We slouch on the couch in a big, comfy nest!
We talk through our day and get things off our chest.
We figure stuff out while we're getting some rest.

In this room we clean,
but we never just clean.....

We make funny faces and try to look mean!
We paint works of art that will never be seen.
We work through our worries
as well as get clean.

In this room we sleep,
    but we never just sleep . . . .

We hide under pillows and don't make a peep.
We build giant castles and count fluffy sheep.
We comfort each other at night before sleep.

In this house we play,
but we never **just play** . . . .

We clean up the mess at the end of the day.
We learn to say sorry and wipe tears away.
We love every minute, at home, when we play.

...I wonder if **our house** is something like **yours!**

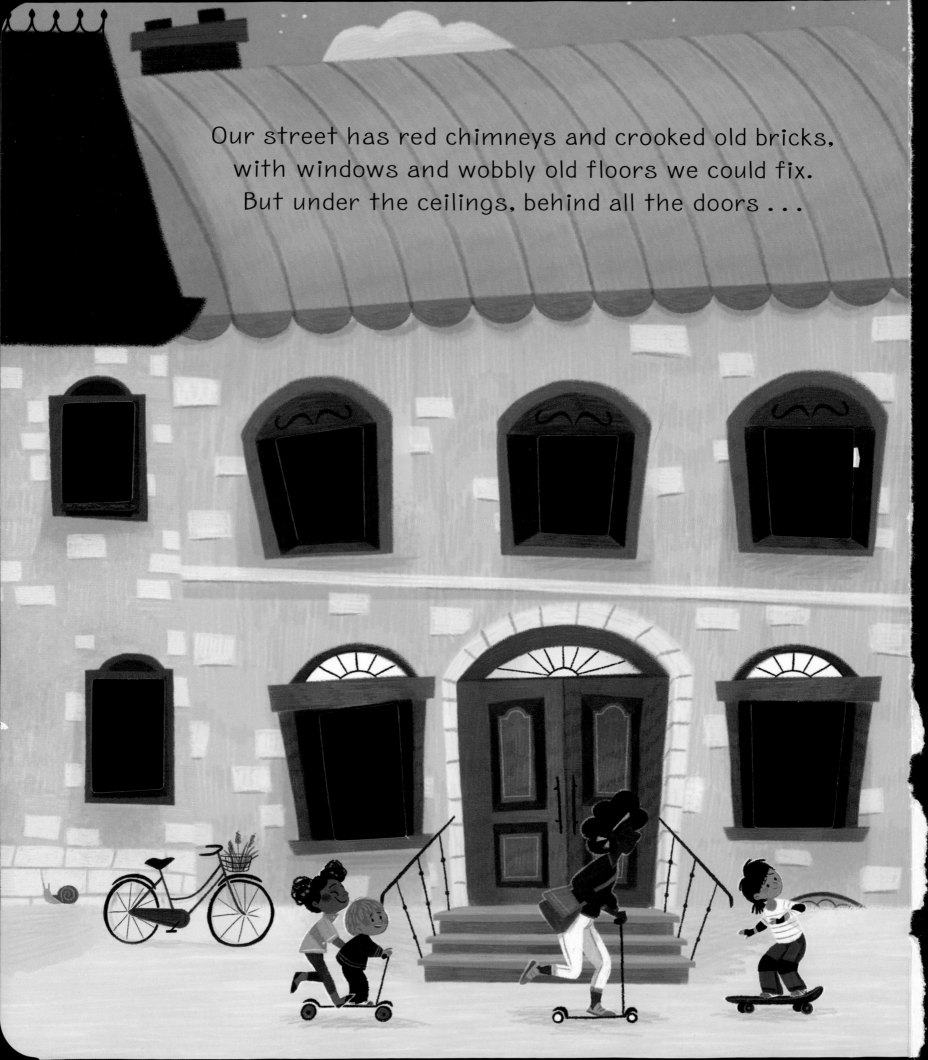

Our street has red chimneys and crooked old bricks,
with windows and wobbly old floors we could fix.
But under the ceilings, behind all the doors . . .